Albany Public Library
Albany, NY

AUG 1 8 2021

W9-AHY-944

For my dear
grandchildren:
Although we can't
always be together
in person,
my love is always
with you —S.B.

For G-Ma
and Lucy —D.Y.

ONE, TWO, GRANDMA LOVES YOU

words by
Shelly Becker

pictures by
Dan Yaccarino

ABRAMS APPLESEED · NEW YORK

One, two, Grandma loves you.

Three, four, visit more.

Five, six,
precious pics.

Seven, eight, mark the date.

Nine, ten, together again!

One, two, Grandma loves you.

Three, four, best toy store.

Five, six, measure and mix.

Seven, eight, stay up late.

Nine, ten, all tucked in!

One, two, Grandma loves you.

Three, four, blocking door.

Five, six,
a few more pics.

Seven, eight,
swinging gate.

Nine, ten, come again!

One, two, Grandma loves you.

Three, four, phone more.

Five, six,
brand-new pics.

Seven, eight,
hang them straight.

Nine, ten, plan again . . .

. . . one, two,
Grandma loves you!

THE ARTWORK
FOR THIS BOOK
WAS CREATED
DIGITALLY.

ABRAMS The Art of Books
195 Broadway, New York, NY 10007
abramsbooks.com

Library of Congress Control Number 2020949263
ISBN 978-1-4197-4218-7

Text © 2021 Shelly Becker
Illustrations © 2021 Dan Yaccarino
Book design by Hana Anouk Nakamura

Published in 2021 by Abrams Appleseed, an imprint
of ABRAMS. All rights reserved. No portion of this
book may be reproduced, stored in a retrieval
system, or transmitted in any form or by any
means, mechanical, electronic, photocopying,
recording, or otherwise, without written
permission from the publisher.

Abrams Appleseed® is a registered
trademark of Harry N. Abrams, Inc.

Printed and bound in China
10 9 8 7 6 5 4 3 2 1

For bulk discount inquiries,
contact specialsales@abramsbooks.com.